"I've Seen Granddad"

Class

Leabharl

Ní mór a
ar nó roin

Ar iarratas
athnuacha

Gearrfa
choime

by June Duffy

Introduction

Ireland will always have a special place in my heart. From the first day that I came over with Tony, who is now my husband, I felt I had discovered a magical, mystical home. The beauty of the countryside and the friendliness of the people still make this home complete for me. It seemed a natural step to combine my love of Ireland with my passion for writing story poems.

So...here is the first of what I know will be several stories. Based in the West of Ireland, and in particular around the bog, the story gives a snapshot of a family and their life. As the story unfolds, many questions will arise and it will be for you, the reader, to decide what really happens. Isn't that just like life anyways?

I hope you enjoy the story. Happy reading.

- June Duffy

I was born on my Granddad's
birthday and this book is
dedicated to his memory.
Hugh Henry William Underhill.

"I've seen Granddad", sang Séan
as he bounced through the door,

His coat tumbling down
by the rug on the floor

"He's been stacking the turf
on the bog all day,

And he's coming
to talk with Dad. Okay?"

Mammy Kathleen stood still,
gave Séan one of her looks.

Said, "Now Séan settle
and take out your school books.

It's time to be doing
your homework, young lad,

Not dreaming of seeing
your old Granddad."

"Not dreaming", Séan shouted
"I know it's true.

I saw him as clearly
as I'm seeing you!"

Just then his two sisters
came in home from school.

Saw their young brother's face
screwing into a ball.

"S'up Séanie?" Mary
the eldest enquired.

Out tumbled the story,
just as it had transpired.

His sisters then laughed
'til tears started to stream.

"Aw Séanie," said Lizzie,
"You're such a scream!"

"Girls stop teasing", said Mammy Kathleen
"He's just a baby of four.

Go easy now. He really believes
it was his old Granddad he saw".

The garden gate creaked open and shut.
"It's Dad", whispered all three...

"He's talking with someone so hurry up.
They'll be coming in soon for tea".

Two voices were heard to rise and fall
as red stripes fingered the evening air.

Then they faded, drifting down the boreen
as if there'd been no one there.

The strangest sensation
spread round the room,

Like a magic spell cast
by a witch on her broom.

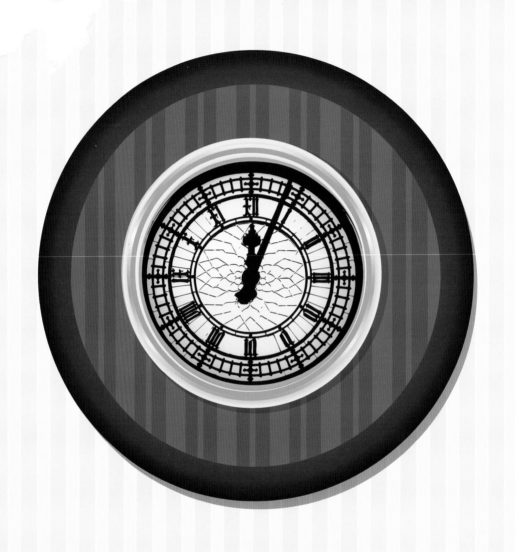

It was just as if time
had been frozen still.

And to make even one move
was against the will.

The spell broke when Mammy Kathleen said
"Let's all get the meal ready then"

"I've seen Granddad" Séan mouthed (but just to himself)
"and I know I will see him again".

"I've Seen Granddad"
 by June Duffy

Memories of my Granddad

Add a photograph
or drawing of your
Granddad in the frame

His name is _____

His birthday is the _____ of _____

He is the best Granddad ever because _____

_____